Look for a number 7 on every page!

A catalogue record for this book is available from the British Library.

First edition

Published by Ladybird Books Ltd Loughborough Leicestershire UK
Ladybird Books Inc Auburn Maine 04210 USA

Printed in England (3)

Flick the pages and see me wiggle and giggle.

Funtime 7 for year olds

by Neil and Ting Morris
illustrations by Mike Gordon

Ladybird

Sp●t the difference

How many differences can you spot between these two pictures?

Find the pairs and spot the difference between them.

What's worse than finding a maggot in your apple?

Finding half a maggot!

Keep spotting. There's a 7 on every page.

5

Can you believe it?

Why were the elephants the last to leave the ark?

We had to pack our trunks!

A human body has about 600 muscles. An elephant's trunk has 40,000!

Crickets have ears on their legs.

The longest snake in the world is the python. Amazingly, it can live quite happily on just one meal a year!

On a potato farm in Africa, it was so hot that when the potatoes were dug up they were already cooked and ready to eat!

Shredded wheat was the first breakfast cereal. It was invented about 100 years ago.

No wonder mine's stale!

Have a guess!
Why does the rattlesnake rattle?
1 It's having a chat with a friend.
2 As a warning that it's about to attack.
3 Because it's shivering with fear.

It's raining, it's pouring...
It hasn't rained cats and dogs yet,
but it has rained:
frozen beans in Los Angeles
jellyfish in Melbourne
pilchards in Cardiff
fish in Washington
frogs in Wigan

Some hailstones are as big as footballs!

What a mix up!

These eight characters have got all mixed up. Can you put them right?

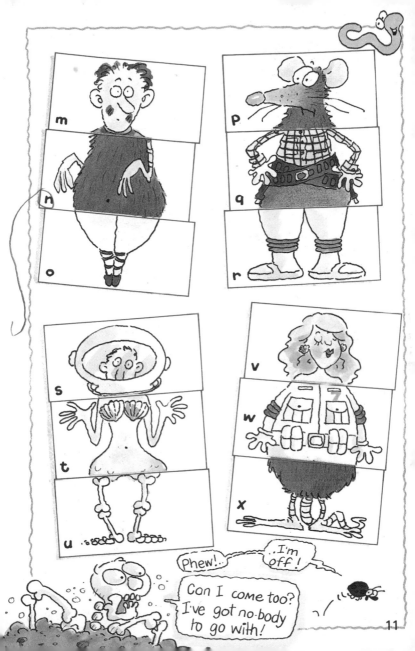

11

It's magic

The disappearing drink stunt

1 I can drink this glass of lemonade without touching the hat!

2 ? Slurp! Slurp! Slurp!

3 Now take the hat off and check.

4 See I drank it without touching the hat!

Matching matches

Make four squares with twelve used matches.

Ask a friend to make the four squares into three squares by moving three matches.

Wow!

Star predictions

1. Ask each person in the audience to name a famous pop star. Write the name down on a slip of paper. Fold the slips up and put them in your magic hat.

2. Ask someone to take out one of the slips and keep it.

3. Tear up all the other slips in the hat and throw them away.

4. Concentrate "magically" on the one which has been taken out.

5. Now name the pop star written on the slip of paper.

6. The person holding the slip will be amazed – you are right!

The secret:

Write down only the first pop star named on every slip of paper. That's the answer!

Did you hear about the sword swallower? on a diet? ...

.. He only eats knives!

13

Fancy that!

These animals are going to a fancy dress party. They have all swapped faces. Which animal is behind each mask?

15

Tongue twisters

Say these tongue twisters quickly
and as many times as you can —
before you go round the twist!

I've got a black-backed
bath brush.

The sun shines on shop signs.

The sixth sheikh's sixth sheep's sick.

Yikes!

Thin sticks. Thick bricks.

Silly rhymes...

There was a young man of Devizes
Whose ears were of different sizes.
The one that was small
Was no use at all,
But the other won several prizes.

There was an old woman
Who swallowed a fly.
I don't know why she swallowed a fly,
Perhaps she'll die...

What did the old woman say after she swallowed the fly?

Burp!

There was a young man of St Just
Who ate apple pie till he bust.
It wasn't the fruit
That caused him to do it;
What finished him off
was the crust.

17

☙ Haunted Hotel ☙

The ghosts are playing **Haunt-and-Seek**.
There are thirteen ghosts hidden at the
Haunted Hotel. Can you find them?

What did the mother ghost say when her son went out to play?

...Don't get your sheet dirty!

Gulp!

Haunted Hotel
☙ Scare away menu ☙
Scream of mushroom
Soup
Ghoul - ash
Beings on toast
Dreaded Wheat
I - scream
Slime Juice.

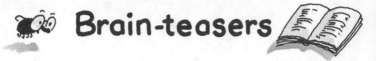

Brain-teasers

These objects are quite ordinary, but they have been drawn from unusual angles. Can you tell what they are?

1

2

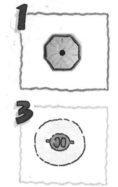

3

4

How many knots must you untie to make this piece of rope straight?

Be careful it's tricky.

Clever riddles

1. What has a tongue but can't talk?

2. What can speak every language in the world?

3. What can't you name without breaking it?

4. What falls without hurting itself?

5. What gets wetter the more it dries?

6. What can run but has no legs?

7. What always ends everything?

8. Which is heavier, a kilo of apples or a kilo of feathers?

If you have six sweets and your sister asks for two, how many will you be left with?

Six — I wouldn't give her any!

Animal quiz

1 Cats have nine lives.

2 Tortoises are the longest-living animals.

3 All cats have the same number of whiskers.

4 Turtles have no teeth.

5 Dinosaurs laid eggs.

6 Moles can see in the dark.

7 Cats can't swim.

8 Skunks smell.

9 Very rich pigs live in sty-scrapers.

10 Snakes have no ears.

11 Turkeys come from Turkey.

Busy Bear has made friends at the beach. Look at the picture carefully for a minute. Then cover it up and see if you can answer the questions at the bottom of the page.

1 How many bears in the picture?

2 How many spades are in the red bucket?

3 What colour are Busy Bear's swimming trunks?

4 How many towers on the sandcastle?

5 What is Busy Bear doing?

23

Crazy cartoons

What do these dotty doodles show?

Teacher: *What's the outside layer of a tree called?*
Billy: *Don't know.*
Teacher: *Bark, Billy!*
Billy: *Woof, woof!*

Woof, woof.

Teacher: *If I gave you three hamsters today and then two tomorrow, how many would you have?*
Billy: *Seven.*
Teacher: *Seven?*
Billy: *Yes, I've got two already.*

Son: *I don't want to go to school today, Mum.*
Mum: *But you must, dear.*
Son: *Nobody likes me. I hate school. Can't I stay home?*
Mum: *No, you are the teacher!*

Hee, hee, hee, hee.

Silly riddles

Ten cats were in a boat. One jumped out.
How many were left?

None. They were copycats.

Which side of an apple pie is the left side?

The one that hasn't been eaten.

Three men fell into the water, but only two
men got their hair wet. Why?

One was bald.

Why do bees hum?

I don't know!

What is black and white and red all over?

A zebra blushing.

What starts with T, ends with T and is
full of T?

Teapot.

Here's a good game to play with a friend. Look at each other and see which one can *buzz-zz-z-z-z-z-z-z* the longest.

BUZZZZZZZZzzzz

Why do cows wear cowbells?

Because their horns don't work.

Why is mayonnaise never ready?

Because it's always dressing.

What is white and flies upwards?

A stupid snowflake.

Because we don't know the words!

What flowers grow between your nose and your chin?

Tulips.

Why can't anyone fool me?...

I've got no leg to pull!

Two oranges were rolling down a hill, but one stopped. Why?

It had run out of juice!

Ha! Ha! Ha!

ANSWERS

Page 4: In the bottom picture: the scarecrow is missing; the fork has gained a middle prong; the farmer has a different hat; the hen has laid a square egg; the horse has zebra stripes; the sun is not smiling; the window is not broken; one of the piglets has changed to a dog; the farmer has a pocket in his shirt; and the fence does not have a crossbar

Page 5: One clown has two spots on his hat, the other has three; one seal is riding on a spotty ball, the other ball has stars; one apple has a maggot in it; one car has an aerial; and one cat has four whiskers, the other has five

Page 9: A rattlesnake rattles as a warning that it's about to attack

Pages 10/11: Characters: gorilla (a, h, f); skeleton (d, b, u); ballerina (g, k, o); cowboy (j, q, i); footballer (m, e, c); mouse (p, n, x); astronaut (s, w, r): and mermaid (v, t, l)

Page 12 (bottom): Matching matches

Pages 14/15: Monkey with elephant mask; mouse with frog mask; zebra with giraffe mask; rhino with monkey mask; tiger with crocodile mask; giraffe with tiger mask; pelican with zebra mask; elephant with pelican mask; frog with mouse mask; and crocodile with rhino mask

Page 20 (top): 1 the end of a pencil; **2** an egg; **3** a light bulb; **4** an iron

Page 20 (bottom): You must untie six knots to make the rope straight

Page 21: 1 a shoe; **2** an echo; **3** silence; **4** rain; **5** a towel; **6** a nose; **7** the letter G; **8** they both weigh the same – a kilo!

Page 22: 1 false; **2** true; **3** false; **4** true; **5** true; **6** false; **7** false; **8** true; **9** false; **10** true; **11** false

Page 23: 1 six; **2** two; **3** white; **4** six; **5** fishing

Page 24: 1 eight Mexicans standing in a circle; **2** a Mexican frying an egg; **3** a cat hiding behind a rock; **4** a jumping bean; **5** a giraffe passing a window; **6** a duck drinking out of a bucket; **7** a thin dog passing a gap in the fence